# BEAR ISLAND

By Katharine Ross

Illustrated by Lisa McCue

Random House New York

Text copyright © 1987 by Random House, Inc. Illustrations copyright © 1987 by Lisa McCue. All rights reserved under International and Pan-American Copyright Conventions. Published in the United States by Random House, Inc., New York, and simultaneously in Canada by Random House of Canada Limited, Toronto. Library of Congress Catalog Card Number: 86-62114   ISBN: 0-394-88631-3   Manufactured in Singapore   1 2 3 4 5 6 7 8 9 0

Two friends, a bear and a rabbit, built a boat.
They built it out of little bits of this and that
and hunks of driftwood that had washed up on
the beach.

When the boat was all finished, Bear said,
"Anchors aweigh—what do you say?"

Rabbit hung back. "Let's not." For rabbits,
as everybody knows, don't take much to water.

"Don't worry," said Bear. "I will protect you.
I will be captain and you will be my first mate."

"Aye–aye, Captain," said Rabbit.

So they set sail with the tide.

It was splendid at sea. Even Rabbit enjoyed himself. The sun sparkled on the water, the tangy breezes caressed their whiskers, and there was always lots to eat: seaweed rolls and briny shrimp and, once in a while, a ripe coconut that bobbed by.

At night the moon rose, bigger and brighter than they had ever seen it from land. Bear strummed his ukulele and sang while Rabbit, sleepy and contented, lay on his back and blinked up at the stars.

After many days at sea Rabbit said, "I miss the land."

Bear said, "Me too, friend. Let's find ourselves an island."

They sailed past an island where there was nothing but raccoons.

"Not here," said Rabbit. "They'd make us wash too often."

They sailed past an island where there was nothing but frogs.

"Too noisy," said Bear, shaking his head.

They sailed past an island where there were only skunks.

Everyone knows why they did not land there!

That afternoon Bear spied great, dark storm clouds piling up on the horizon.

Rabbit's nose twitched. "I smell a storm!"

Sure enough, a howling gale blew up. It soaked the decks and tattered the sail and tossed the friends topsy-turvy.

Then a great, huge, tremendous wave picked them up and hurled them high into the air.

They landed on a beach with a bump.

"Oh!" said Rabbit.

"My!" said Bear. "What have we here?"

Their boat lay about them on the sand in little bits and pieces.

"We'd better get started building another," said Rabbit.

"Not now," said Bear. "Let's explore."

And explore they did.

Bear blazed trails. Rabbit made a basket and collected specimens, for he was an avid naturalist.

Out of the pieces of their wrecked boat they built a hut right on the beach. There was a place to sleep, a place to cook and eat, and a place to entertain guests.

That night, as they were falling asleep, Rabbit said, "Let's stay—what do you say?"

"Oh, I was hoping you'd say that," said Bear. "I like it here too. Let's call it Rabbit and Bear Island."

"Too long," said Rabbit, shaking his head.

"How about Friendship Island?"

"Too stuffy," said Rabbit. "How about Bear Island?"

"But you live here too!" Bear protested.

"Yes," said Rabbit with a smile. "But I wouldn't if it weren't for you."

So Bear Island it was. And on Bear Island they stayed in peace and happiness for many years.

And Bear Island came to be known far and wide as the most wonderful place to visit.